WARNING!

Scaredy Squirrel insists that everyone put on earmuffs before reading this book.

For Maxime, Marc-Olivier, Thomas, Cédric, Victoria,
Simon, Guillaume, Camille, Jérôme, Louis, Maude,
Janique and Romeo

Text and illustrations © 2011 Mélanie Watt

Kids Can Press acknowledges the financial support of the Government of Ontario, through the Ontario
Media Development Corporation's Ontario Book Initiative; the Ontario Arts Council; the Canada Council
for the Arts; and the Government of Canada, through the CBF, for our publishing activity.

Published in Canada by
Kids Can Press Ltd.
25 Dockside Drive
Toronto, ON M5A 0B5

Published in the U.S. by
Kids Can Press Ltd.
2250 Military Road
Tonawanda, NY 14150

www.kidscanpress.com

The artwork in this book was rendered digitally in Photoshop.
The text is set in Potato Cut.

Edited by Tara Walker
Designed by Mélanie Watt and Karen Powers

The hardcover edition of this book is smyth sewn casebound.
The paperback edition of this book is limp sewn with a drawn-on cover.
Manufactured in Tseung Kwan O, NT Hong Kong, China, in 6/2014 by Paramount Printing Co. Ltd.

CM 11 0 9 8 7 6 5 4 3
CM PA 14 0 9 8 7 6 5 4 3 2

LIBRARY AND ARCHIVES CANADA CATALOGUING IN PUBLICATION

Watt, Mélanie, 1975–
    Scaredy Squirrel has a birthday party / Mélanie Watt.

ISBN 978-1-55453-468-5 (bound)   ISBN 978-1-55453-716-7 (pbk.)

    1. Squirrels — Juvenile fiction. 2. Picture books for children.
3. Birthdays — Juvenile fiction. 4. Birthday parties — Juvenile fiction.   I. Title.

PS8645.A8845283 2011   jC813'.6   C2010-905528-4

Kids Can Press is a *corus*™ Entertainment company

Scaredy Squirrel

has a birthday party

by Mélanie Watt

KIDS CAN PRESS

Scaredy Squirrel never has big birthday parties. He'd rather celebrate alone quietly up in his tree than party below and risk being taken by surprise.

A few surprises
Scaredy Squirrel
is afraid could
spoil the party:

clownfish

ants

Bigfoot

confetti

ponies

porcupines

So he plans a small celebration where he's the only life of the party.

BIRTHDAY PARTY CHECKLIST

A) Confirm date of birth ☑

B) Pick a safe location ☑

C) Choose party colors ☑

D) Get tuxedo dry-cleaned ☑

E) Prepare cake recipe ☑

F) Practice breathing ☑
(to blow up balloons/blow out candles)

G) Mail party invitation to myself ☐

EXHIBIT A

BIRTH CERTIFICATE

This certifies that __SCAREDY ORVILLE SQUIRREL__

was born on _____OCTOBER 3RD_____

at this time _1:28 AND 6 SECONDS_ in _NUT TREE_.

Weight_14.8_ grams   Height_8.24_ cm

Cute_YES_   Teeth_NO_   Fleas_NO_

Left paw print

Right paw print

OFFICIAL IMPORTANT RODENT DOCUMENT

EXHIBIT B

EXHIBIT C

EXHIBIT D

221

EXHIBIT E

-NUTTY CAKE RECIPE-

2 cups flour
1 cup brown sugar
1 tsp. baking soda
1 tsp. baking powder
½ tsp. salt
1 egg
1 cup milk
¼ cup canola oil
8 cups nuts (1 cup for non-rodents)

SCAREDY SQUIRREL'S BAKING INSTRUCTIONS:
Preheat oven to 348.9°F and keep fire extinguisher nearby.
Verify expiration dates on all ingredients
Mix the dry ingredients then add egg, milk and oil. Do not forget the nuts! Stir clockwise.
Pour carefully into greased pan. Bake for precisely 49 minutes and 32 seconds.
Put on heavy-duty oven mitts and remove from oven.
Let cool and decorate (make it pleasing to the eye).

EXHIBIT F

EXHIBIT G

SCAREDY'S BREATHING CHART

PERFECT

GOOD

OKAY

1 2 3 4 5 6 7 8 9 10 (No. of tries)

Scaredy

YOU'RE INVITED TO SCAREDY SQUIRREL'S BIRTHDAY PARTY!

When? Today at 1:00 p.m.
Where? Nut tree, Unknown Ave.

○ YES, I CAN
○ NO, I CAN'T — I HAVE TO WASH MY FUR

Scaredy Squirrel heads down to mail his invitation. He pauses when he spots a card tucked inside his mailbox.

ROSES ARE RED,
VIOLETS ARE BLUE,
I JUST HAD TO BE
THE FIRST TO WISH A
HAPPY BIRTHDAY
TO YOU!

Sincerely,
Buddy

Scaredy gives it some thought.
He decides that a kindly gesture
deserves a kindly response.

So he changes the invitation ...

Scaredy 's BUDDY

YOU'RE INVITED TO
SCAREDY SQUIRREL'S
BIRTHDAY PARTY!

When? Today at 1:00 p.m.
Where? Nut tree, Unknown Ave.

◯ YES, I CAN
◯ NO, I CAN'T — I HAVE TO WASH MY FUR

But inviting a guest
is one risky move!

 A few last-minute items Scaredy needs to throw a party at ground level:

safety goggles

carrot

deck of cards

earmuffs

cookies

Beethoven statue

rented party tent

fishing rod

BIRTHDAY (PARTY OF 2) PLAN

Send invitation to Buddy on the fly!

Buddy

Party was up here.

Party is moving down here.

To avoid being taken for a ride, attach carrot to fishing rod to lure away ponies.

Bigfoot is a huge party crasher! Build a house of cards so he stomps on that instead of the tent.

Confetti gets out of control. Keep it away by celebrating under cover!

Clownfish have tricks up their sleeves and are no laughing matter! Humor them with a hard-headed guest who will never crack a smile.

Ants are no picnic — they eat everything in their path. These party poopers will hit the road when they come across a tasty trail of cookies!

Porcupines and balloons: need I say more? If disaster pops up, think fast — put on goggles and earmuffs!

Note to self: If all else fails, play dead and cancel the party!

IMPORTANT! The secret to a successful party is all in the details!

DETAIL 1: SELECT CONVERSATION TOPICS FOR SMALL TALK

GOOD IDEA

BAD IDEA

How about that great weather we've been having?

Before we shake paws ... have you been checked for fleas?

So, do you come here often?

They say mints help fight bad breath. Pssst! Be my guest!

If you were a tree, what type of tree would you be?

Is that a muskrat on your head? Oops ... it's a toupee.

DETAIL 2: DETERMINE THE DOs AND DON'Ts OF PARTYING

DO

DON'T

EAT TOO MANY SWEETS

LISTEN TO LOUD MUSIC

SURPRISE THE BIRTHDAY SQUIRREL

BREAK DANCE

SPILL ANYTHING

DOUBLE-DIP

SIT QUIETLY

PLAY PINATA GAMES

DETAIL 3: PREPARE A BIRTHDAY PARTY SCHEDULE

Time	Task	
1:00 p.m.	Serve punch	
1:01 p.m.	Look out for:	
1:03 p.m.	Serve dip	
1:06 p.m.	Brush teeth	
1:09 p.m.	Make small talk	
1:19 p.m.	Play a quiet game of dominos	
1:24 p.m.	Look out for:	
1:26 p.m.	Locate fire extinguisher	

1:27 p.m.	Bring out cake	
1:28 p.m.	Take a breath and blow out candle	
1:29 p.m.	Look out for:	
1:31 p.m.	Eat cake	
1:35 p.m.	Brush teeth	
1:38 p.m.	Read thank-you speech	
1:40 p.m.	Look out for:	
1:42 p.m.	Sit quietly	
2:00 p.m.	The party's over	
2:01 p.m.	Start planning next year's birthday	

Step by step, Scaredy Squirrel carefully prepares for his party. Everything is perfect, right down to the last detail.

GERM-FREE PARTY

But at 1:00 p.m. . . .

This was NOT part of the Plan!

HAPPY BIRTHDAY!

GERM-FREE PARTY

Scaredy Squirrel panics!

He scatters ...

SIT!

He stops the music ...

He chases . . .

He screams . . .

He ducks . . .

He freezes and . . .

Scaredy Squirrel finally opens his eyes.

He sees that his birthday cake is lit and everyone is sitting quietly.

Scaredy blows out
his birthday candle.
He forgets all about the
clownfish, ants, Bigfoot,
confetti, ponies and
porcupines.

This party is going
to be a piece of cake!

Afterward, Scaredy Squirrel receives something unexpected.

FOR:
SCAREDY

A BIRTHDAY PRESENT

Inside, Scaredy finds a special surprise ...

elegant wood-finish frame

oak tree interpretation

handsome squirrel portrait

some sort of purple unidentified flying object thingy

puppy signatures

heartwarming symbol of affection

Scaredy gives it some thought.
He decides that a kindly gesture
deserves a kindly response.

So he changes next year's
invitation ...

Scaredy's BUDDY Plus: Pecan,
Cashew,
Peanut,
Hazel,
Coco,
Pinenut,
Pistachio,
Mack and
Damian

YOU'RE INVITED TO
SCAREDY SQUIRREL'S
BIRTHDAY PARTY!

→next year
When? Today at 1:00 p.m.
Where? Nut tree, Unknown Ave.

○ YES, I CAN
○ NO, I CAN'T — I HAVE TO WASH MY FUR

NEXT YEAR'S BIRTHDAY PARTY CHECKLIST

A) Confirm date of birth ☐

B) Rent larger party tent ☐

C) Choose party colors ☐

D) Dress casual ☐

E) Bake bigger cake ☐

F) Practice breathing to calm down ☐

G) Shrink-wrap everything ☐

H) Buy dog biscuits ☐

M) Put on good sneakers ☐

N) Wear top-of-the-line earplugs ☐

O) Buy toothbrushes in bulk ☐

P) Get a Frisbee ☐

Q) Install hand-sanitizer dispenser ☐

U) Rent porta-potty ☐

V) Prepare doggy bags ☐

W) Memorize the speech ☐

P.S. This birthday party left Scaredy Squirrel speechless.

thank-you speech